Professor P. and Morrison—
they find the rope ladder
and the map of
the Island of Elves

Rolypoly—
he likes
the fresh air

Dr. Pleasant—
a sympathetic
listener

The Newspaper Reader—
he's very concerned
about all the disasters
he reads about
in the newspaper

Parson Plump

The Terrorist

Super Sleuth
Hawkeye

The Twins

The World's
Unluckiest Man

The World's
Second
Unluckiest Man

Little Blue Top

Mr. Brown—
kind and helpful

Doomsday Prophet—
he's always predicting
the end of the world

The four card players

Mr. Kindheart

Nimble and Fumble

Mex

Whitebeard

Piggy and Peckish

*Dull and Dreary—
they think
everything is boring*

Sleepy and his two pests

The fifteen extra characters

Jan Mogensen
The 46 Little Men

Puffin Books

PUFFIN BOOKS
Published by the Penguin Group
Penguin Books USA Inc., 375 Hudson Street, New York, New York 10014, U.S.A.
Penguin Books Ltd, 27 Wrights Lane, London W8 5TZ, England
Penguin Books Australia Ltd, Ringwood, Victoria, Australia
Penguin Books Canada Ltd, 10 Alcorn Avenue, Toronto, Ontario, Canada M4V 3B2
Penguin Books (N.Z.) Ltd, 182–190 Wairau Road, Auckland 10, New Zealand

Penguin Books Ltd, Registered Offices: Harmondsworth, Middlesex, England

First published in Denmark by Munksgaard A/S, 1990
First published in the United States of America by Greenwillow Books,
a division of William Morrow & Company, Inc., 1991
Reprinted by arrangement with William Morrow & Company, Inc.
Published in Puffin Books, 1993
1   3   5   7   9   10   8   6   4   2
Copyright © Munksgaard and Jan Mogensen, 1990
All rights reserved

LIBRARY OF CONGRESS CATALOGING-IN-PUBLICATION DATA
Mogensen, Jan.
[46 små mænd. English]
The 46 little men / Jan Mogensen.   p.   cm.
Translation of: De 46 små mænd.
Summary: Relates, in wordless illustrations, the adventures of the
forty-six little men who live in the picture on the nursery wall.
ISBN 0-14-054831-9
[1. Stories in rhyme.]   I. Title.   II. Title: Forty-six little men.
[PZ7.M7274Aag 1993]   [E]—dc20   92-25329

Printed in the United States of America
Set in Benguiat Gothic

The 46 Little Men

Forty-six little men—forty-six stories!

The forty-six little men live in a picture on the nursery wall. One day Professor P. and his friend Morrison open the brown suitcase and find two nails, a rope ladder, and a map of the Island of the Elves....

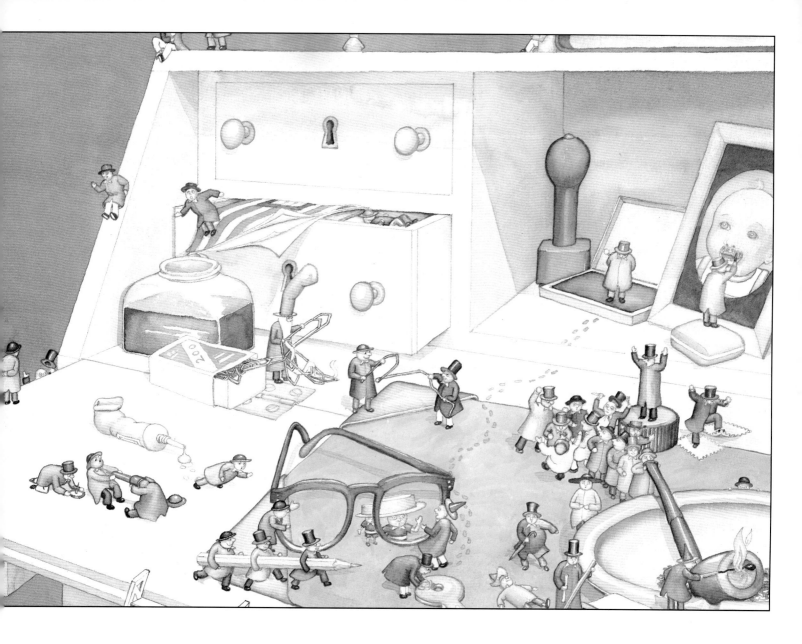

Professor P. and Morrison—
they find the rope ladder
and the map of
the Island of Elves

Rolypoly—
he likes
the fresh air

Dr. Pleasant—
a sympathetic
listener

The Newspaper Reader—
he's very concerned
about all the disasters
he reads about
in the newspaper

Parson Plump

The Terrorist

Super Sleuth
Hawkeye

The Twins

The World's
Unluckiest Man

The World's
Second
Unluckiest Man

Little Blue Top

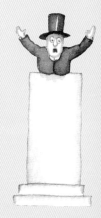

Mr. Brown—
kind and helpful

Doomsday Prophet—
he's always predicting
the end of the world

The four card players

Mr. Kindheart

Nimble and Fumble

Mex

Whitebeard

Piggy and Peckish

Dull and Dreary—
they think
everything is boring

Sleepy and his two pests

The fifteen extra characters